The Fate of the Future

The Chronicles of Fuamahoya

Book 1

By Marisa Avery

Dedicated to

My wonderful mother, (Kim), who helped me along, not letting me give up.

And to

Mrs. Mobley, who encouraged me to keep writing, and got excited about each new chapter.

Thank you both.

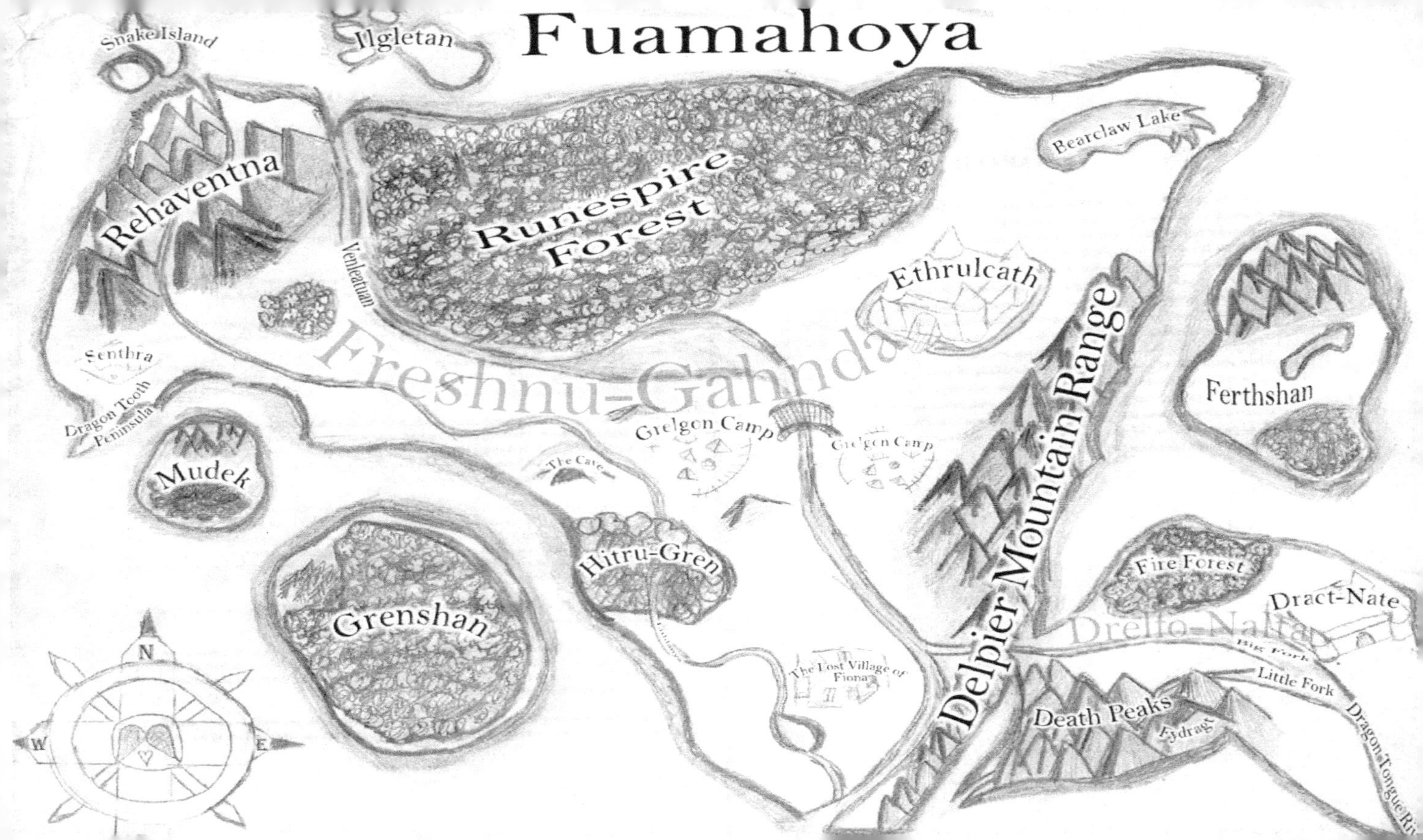
Fuamahoya
Snake Island
Ilgletan
Rehaventna
Runespire Forest
Venleatuan
Bearclaw Lake
Ethrulcath
Freshnu-Gahnda
Delpier Mountain Range
Ferthshan
Senthra
Dragon Tooth Peninsula
Mudek
Grelgen Camp
Grelgen Camp
The Cave
Hitru-Gren
Grenshan
The Lost Village of Fiona
Fire Forest
Dract-Nate
Drelfo-Nalta
Big Fork
Little Fork
Death Peaks
Fydragt
Dragon Tongue Riv
N
W
E

Table of Contents

Prologue: The End Has Just Begun

The long awaited time has arrived. Lanthiraya smiled. Soon, very soon, the whole of Fuamahoya would be *hers*. She would be ruler of ALL of Fuamahoya…

Suddenly, a shout erupted throughout the hall, and the Grelgon queen narrowed her eyes. Who *dare* disturb her? She glared with annoyance at the door to her throne room and almost jumped as it was flung open, slamming against the wall with a *BANG!*

"Your Majesty!" the Grelgon cried, bending down into a deep bow. "Reports of suspicious and important activity among the human race our spy has just brought back," he said, rising up to glance at her face.

"Yes?" she asked in a deadly smooth voice.

"The humans…..have gotten stronger…they have a …power…that can resist our attacks...the gods have joined forces with the humans…if we do not act soon…we will be wiped from Fuamahoya and existence entirely," he said. "There is also a prophecy…" he stopped, waiting to see her reaction.

"What is it about?" she asked icily.

The Grelgon cleared his throat and began to recite:

"The day the night falls when the moon should lie,

The day that the stars from the sky,

The day when the evil green ones invade,

The humans shall hearken to the price they have paid,

A silver haired woman shall bring forth the child

Driving the evil into its lair,

Making the kingdom whole, reveal the lost heir,

Saving the world, the green ones are exiled."

He stopped, and coughed, watching the queens face.

"Hmm..." Lanthiraya said, digesting this information. "Leave me! I must think…" she commanded.

The Grelgon scrambled from the room, shutting the door behind him.

Lanthiraya gazed out the window at the mountains…*Fydragt. Death Mountains...Fire Fury…Death Land...*she thought with a smile. *Only we have named our places after the evil in this world, because we are not afraid of what it can do to us*...She smiled wider. *We will find a way to prevail against this new 'power' the humans have and we WILL take Fuamahoya, once and for all. It may be in a prophecy, but....prophecies can change...*

Lady and Tiger

The clouds hung heavily in the night sky, dimming the light that already was slowly fading. A woman in a dress as dark as the sky itself climbs up the grassy hillside, clutching a dim lantern, which flickers in the cold night air. A small gust of wind blows by, sending a shiver down her spine. She wraps her cloak more tightly around herself, and huddles against the wind. She reaches the top of the hill, and sits down on a small boulder, setting her lantern down next to her. She takes a deep breath and studies the hill around her. White wildflowers grow in clusters all around her feet.

The sound of a quiet growl drifts up the hill. The woman looks up to see an auburn and black striped tiger approach her. On his back, two huge white angel-like wings flutter open and closed, stirring the air around them and making her hair fly. She smiles and holds out her palm to him. He sniffs and nudges it, then she slowly moves her hand up to rest on his soft and furry head. A magic warmth begins to seep through her, and she looks up into the watchful green eyes of her friend.

“Hello, Zeus,” she whispers.

“Greetings, Athena,” Zeus replied. “I wasn’t sure if you would get my message, as I have never used a dove for anything like that before. The only way I see them as useful is as a yummy snack..."

He trailed off, his stomach growling. He smiled timidly, embarrassed. Athena laughed, and soon he joined her. Athena had missed seeing her friend. She thought of all the adventures they could go on now that they were together.

▪▪▪▪▪

"Well," Zeus said suddenly, "I am very glad to see you, and I'm even more excited and intrigued to learn what you have been up to these past few years, but maybe we can do that in a more suitable...and warmer location? Oh, and maybe we can get some dinner too." His stomach rumbled in agreement, and he dipped his head.

Athena laughed and picked up her lantern from where it lay on a nearby rock.

"Of course! I think, if I remember right...there should be a cave nearby, I think I saw it on my way up here. Follow me," she said.

They slowly worked their way down the hillside until they came to a small cave that was half hidden in the grassy slope. Athena went in first, then Zeus. Athena found a small branch and held it out to Zeus. He opened his mouth, and a ball of fire shot out and set the end alight, sending sparks in all directions.

The newly born light illuminated the cave walls, casting their shadows onto the wall. Lady and Tiger. Human and Animal. One pale like the moon, one the color of brittle leaves falling from a tree. In spite of all their differences, they were very much alike.

Athena looked around the cave and then wedged the end of the makeshift torch into a crack in the cave wall. She sat down on a small rock and pulled her pack off her back. She unfastened the top and rummaged through the contents, arranging it all out on the rough rock floor, and mentally checking each item off on her list. *Hunting knife*, she thought, placing it on the floor next to her tightly folded blanket. She pulled out a small canteen and set it on top of her blanket. An extra pair of wool gloves. A small bottle, filled with healing ointment. She went through until she was sure she hadn't forgotten anything. Satisfied, she begins picking up all of her supplies and putting them neatly back into the tan leather pack. Then she pushed the pack over by the wall and stood up, stretching. She grabbed her bow and her quiver of arrows fletched with green and white feathers and slung them over her back. Zeus stood up and joined her as she reached the entrance to their cave.

"Going hunting?" he asked.

"Yes. I want to get something to eat before dusk," she replied. "You can stay here in the cave if you want...or you can come with me."

"I'll come," he responded. "After all, I know a spot where there is a group of unsuspecting prey"

"Okay, I'm going to go into the woods and try to get a rabbit or two. Maybe three. But you can go...do whatever...you said you were going to do, I guess?" Athena replied. "Whatever. Just don't get lost, and be back here before dark, I want to stay dry tonight."

Zeus chuckled softly. "Okay, I will go scout out my meal and then I'll meet you here at...."

"Just come back whenever you feel like you have whatever you need," she waited a moment, then added, "And I will do the same."

Athena smiled, then she ducked out of the cave. Outside, she paused and inhaled the cool crisp air, the scent of the wildflowers on the wind. She heard the roar of thunder in the distance, which meant that they should move quickly if they wanted to get something to eat before the clouds *really* opened up on them. As she stepped into the maze of wood, her hunters' instincts kicked in automatically. She softly crept forward, on silent feet, carefully stepping around the patches of leaves and puddles of water, so as not to make any sound. She heard the rustle of leaves and in an instant her bow was loaded, aimed at an innocent-looking blackberry bush.

A Thousand Eyes

After a few moments of quiet, she decided that it must have been a bird or something. That was fine. The berries would be good to eat even without anything else. Looking around, her eyes fell on a small tree branch, heavily weighted down with oddly shaped crimson-colored leaves. Well, at least she thought they were leaves. Never having seen the kind of tree before, she didn't really know. She stepped closer, examining the small, delicate red teardrops. Yes, they were some kind of waxy-looking leaf. Her eyes lifted upward. *Huh.* She pulled off a few of them and wrapped them in the normal green leaves of a maple tree, sticking the bundle into her game bag. She would look at it more closely later. Judging from the waxy-ness of the leaves, they were probably flammable, a theory she could have Zeus help her with. For now, though, she needed to get some food, and fast, because the sky was getting darker by the minute, and the storm was getting closer too. She ventured farther into the vast green canopy.

▪▪▪▪▪

Five minutes later she was weaving through the thicket of dark green foliage, trying not to make a sound as she swiftly followed the fat gray rabbit that had caught her attention. She'd been on its trail for three minutes now. The rabbit stopped, interested in a clump of leaves that was hanging off of a blackberry bush, heavy with fruit. Athena stopped, silently raised her bow, the arrow drawn back, aimed for the rabbit's head. Waiting... *SNAP!*

Athena nearly jumped when she heard the sound of a twig snapping, out of the corner of her eye she saw the rabbit's head shoot up, looking to a spot at Athena's left. It stayed completely still for about five seconds, then it shot into the weeds, disappearing. *SNAP!* Another twig snapped. Athena looked in the direction of the sound and saw a small brown doe grazing on the small tufts of grass poking through the layer of leaves on the ground. She was maybe 3 years old, with small white dots scattered on her. Athena crept forward with a velvet tread, not wanting to scare her away. She reached a thicket that was overgrown enough to hide her and crouched down, lifting her arrow to the deer. She was about to release the arrow when a second deer came bounding out of the trees, slightly smaller than the first one. *A baby deer!* Athena thought. She lowered her bow and stayed crouching, watching the pair silently. The baby had now come over to the mother deer, meeting her at the clump of grass that was so scarce, there were only a few chunks of grass left scattered around the woods.

▪▪▪▪▪

After watching the deer for a good five minutes, Athena decided she had better be getting back to the cave. Slowly, she rose and stretched her cramped muscles. On the way back through the woods, she stopped by the berry bush and gathered as many berries as she could. She popped a few of them in her mouth and felt the delicious taste of the juice spread through her mouth. *Mmm,* Athena thought. *These taste delicious.* They had just the right amount of tartness and sweetness. They would go great with the rabbit she had just shot a few minutes earlier. She even had packed a small loaf of bread, and it was waiting back in her hunting bag in the cave. Something tugged at her memory and she felt a sense of déjà vu. A memory surfaced and she saw herself at a small table, eating toasted bread, cooked rabbit, and berries. Blackberries. She shook herself out of the daze. *What in the world was that?* She did not know what that was all about. She had never remembered anything like that in her life. An uneasy feeling settled over her, making her shiver. After looking around her one last time, she trudged out of the forest, feeling as if there were a thousand pairs of invisible eyes watching her.

Come to Me

Athena got back to the cave in plenty of time. When she slipped through the opening, she saw that Zeus had not gotten back yet. *I'll get dinner ready so that we can eat as soon as he gets here,* she thought. She shivered again as she remembered the strange memory. Maybe she should tell Zeus about it. Maybe he might know what to make of it.

Athena shook her head to clear the thoughts away. *Now is not the time to worry about that. I must make a meal before Zeus gets here,* she thought.

Suddenly there was a bright flash of light before her eyes and she heard a strange voice inside her head: ***Protect the amulet***, it said. ***Do not lose it. Don't trust anyone. Come to me.*** After another flash of light, the voice was gone. Athena shivered and her head spun. She felt like she should lie down. But she had to prepare a meal….

She pulled herself up, and stumbled over to the entrance of the cave, where a small pile of wood had been piled. Grabbing an armful of sticks, she walked back to the middle of the cave and assembled the sticks in a teepee formation. Only then did she realize, she had not packed anything to start a fire with, counting on Zeus to take care of that. *Where is Zeus?* Athena thought. She felt like she hadn't slept in several days. She sighed heavily and crossed over to her pack, barely managing to pull her blanket out before she collapsed onto it and fell asleep.

Adventure Time…

Athena woke to the sound of a crackling fire and the smell of cooking meat. She rolled over and opened her eyes, and almost had a heart attack. Two inches from her face were two large green glowing lamps. *Wait a minute,* she thought. She sat up and was greeted by a welcome sight.

"Well, at least you're awake," Zeus said. "When I came in and saw you lying on the floor, out cold, well, it was the *last* thing I had expected to see, so I *KINDA* freaked out."

Athena smiled weakly. "Well, I wasn't expecting it either." *Protect the amulet.* The voices' words came back to her. *Wait. Amulet? What amulet?* She didn't have an amulet. She felt her neck where there hadn't been anything earlier, and her fingers caught on a pearl necklace. She gasped. She unclasped it and curled it around her fingers, examining it. Purple with swirls of green, blue and hints of red peeking through. Beautiful. It looked ordinary, but it felt like it was vibrating with energy.

"Oh, wow." Zeus said, suddenly materializing beside her. She jumped and he looked at her apologetically. "Sorry, I just happened to look over and see you looking at it. It's quite lovely looking. Though what is strange is, I don't remember you wearing it when you were on the hill and I definitely don't remember you taking it from your hunting bag, although you could have not taken it out on purpose…" he trailed off.

"Zeus, this amulet isn't mine. Until today, I've never seen it." She stopped, remembering what the voice had told her:

Protect the amulet. Do not lose it. Don't trust anyone. Come to me.
She closed her eyes, trying to puzzle out the meaning. 'Don't trust anyone.' Did that include Zeus? He was the only one she'd ever fully trusted. She decided that the voice meant 'anyone you *meet.*' Content, she opened her eyes and opened her mouth. But before she even uttered a word, Zeus shushed her.

"Not yet. I can tell you have a very interesting story to tell me, and I would LOVE to hear it, but first you need to eat something," he declared.

Athena was tempted to argue, but the gnawing in her stomach convinced her otherwise. She started to get up but Zeus's gaze made her sit back down. He brought over a half of the cooked rabbit and a large leaf with some blackberries piled on it. While she ate, he informed her on what had taken him so long to get back.

~

He had been running through the woods, hot on the trail of a very hard to catch, small brown deer, when several twigs snapped a couple of yards to the left of where he was, making him stop. He darted into a thicket of overgrown brush, and seconds later, two men appeared, bearing spears. Upon closer examination, Zeus realized that they were not human. They had pointed ears, long nails, and their skin was green. One of them turned to the other and said in a rough voice: 'Why do we even have to go after them? It's not like they are so special.' The second one replied, 'Because Her Majesty says that the human has a source of power that could destroy us.' It was then that Zeus realized what they were. They were Grelgons. Gorgon-elves. And whoever they were after was not in for a nice chat. The Grelgons were up to no good.

~

Zeus stopped and looked at Athena intensely, waiting, it seemed, for a reaction.

"Wow. So the Grelgons are coming for the humans, and all because of an object of power. Hmmm." Athena trailed off, picking the remains of her rabbit clean.

"Yes, but now you must tell me your story, and I will snack on my ducks while you talk," he said, biting into a roasted duck. He looked at her expectantly.

So she told him everything. About the strange memory she never remembered, about the flash of light and the voice, urgent and cautious, warning her not to trust anybody. About everything that had happened since she'd left the cave and stepped foot in the forest.

Zeus listened intently the whole time Athena was talking, never interrupting once.

"So what do you think all of these things mean?" she asked him, after she'd finished.

He looked at her with a bright look in his eyes. "What do I think?" he echoed mysteriously.
"I think that we have another exciting adventure ahead of us."

…Or Not

Adventure or no adventure, there was no way Athena was going on a wild goose chase to find two Grelgons who could be anywhere by now. And definitely not in the pouring rain that had begun to fall from the sky, matching her mood. She still felt like she'd pulled a huge boulder up a hill, only to have it roll back down.

"Well, you go out adventuring. I am going to stay warm and dry by the fire, and take a nap," Athena said.

Zeus chuckled. "You are silly. I, of course, did not mean we had to go *at the minute.* Rather, I would like to catch a few Z's myself. Oh and maybe some dream food." he added.

Athena laughed. "Zeus, you *just* ate. How can you possibly be hungry again?"

"Well, I get *very* hungry whenever I go on adventures," he said. "And those ducks were *SO* tiny!" he added.

Athena laughed again. She yawned. "I think I should get to sleep. We should get up in the morning as early as we can. To get a good start."

"Yes," Zeus agreed. "Good night, Athena."

"Good night, Zeus." Athena said sleepily.

They both fell asleep, not knowing what the morning would bring, but knowing they would go into it together, as they always have.

A Visit from a God

As soon as her eyes drifted shut, the voice began. ***You must come to me. Bring the amulet. It is the only hope for me. For us. For humankind.***

Athena found herself responding: "Who are you? What is the amulet for? Why do I hear you in my head? Are you real? What is happening to me? Who are you?" She couldn't stop the flow of questions from spewing forth.

"So many questions," the voice chuckled. "However, I suppose it's only fair that you know what you're walking into. So I will answer you, though only sparingly, as I cannot reveal too much, for fear it would make everything go terribly wrong. Do you understand?"

"Yes, I understand," Athena replied.

"Okay, good. Now you may ask me 5 questions, and to start you off, I am Magne, the spirit god." the voice stated.

All of a sudden, Athena found herself standing in a dark cave. A woman, glowing like a lamp in the darkness, was sitting on a rock in front of her. *Is this a dream?* she thought. She stepped forward and sat down across from the glowing woman. The woman, Magne, lifted her head and smiled at Athena.

"Spirit...god?" Athena echoed.

"Yes," Magne said. "I am a god that looks after the spirits roaming the earth."

"Oh," Athena said, "that makes sense."

"Yes," said Magne. "Now, what is your first question that you would like to ask me?"

Athena thought. After a while she asked, "What is happening, and what is the amulet for?"

"Is that one question, or two? No matter, I guess. Ok. Now, there is a great big fight going on between the Grelgons and the humans. The Grelgons, apparently, got wind of the fact that a human has a source of power —"

"— that could destroy them." Athena finished. "That's what it is, it's the amulet, isn't it? That's what they said: '*The human has a source of power that could destroy us.*' But they said *'them'* so that means.... OH!" Athena cut herself off, realizing the answer. "Oh. It's us! It's me and Zeus, isn't it? We are the ones who have to stop it!" she finished breathlessly.

"Well, don't forget me," Magne said, "I'm kind of an important piece to this puzzle too."

Athena smiled. "Do I still get to keep the questions I didn't ask?"

Magne hesitated before she responded. "I suppose so, and I have an idea. Give me your charm bracelet please."

Athena unclasped the tinkling bracelet and passed it to Magne. "Am I still dreaming? Or am I awake?" she asked.

"You are asleep and your tiger friend Zeus is too," Magne replied, closing her eyes. After a few minutes she opened them again and smiled. "Here you are," she said, passing the bracelet back to Athena. "Now, when you are in a tough situation, and you need help, or you have another question, just hold your new charm up and whisper to it: '*Magne, Magne, come to me. I have a question and I will set you free,*' and I will come and help you."

"Thank you so much," Athena said, fastening the bracelet back on her wrist and studying the new question mark shaped charm.

"You are welcome. Now you should get some peaceful sleep before the morning," Magne said with a smile.

"Yes," Athena agreed. "Goodbye! Thank you so much!"

"Good night, Athena." Magne said, snapping her fingers.

Athena was pulled gently from the dream and dropped into heavy darkness. She spun off into uninterrupted sleep, her mind apparently too tired to conjure up dreams.

To Be a Tiger…

Athena stared out at the trees from where she stood at the entrance to the cave, thinking of her dream last night.

“What is on your mind?” Zeus asked, coming up next to her. “I’ve never seen you stand still, or stare at something, for this long.

Athena glanced at him, and saw concern and curiosity in his eyes, which reflected the light coming from inside the cave, turning their normal jade color into a bright emerald shade.

“I was just trying to figure out what we should do,” she said. She waited, taking a deep breath and said, “Zeus, I... I had a…dream…vision, whatever. Last night. It didn’t feel like a dream though…” she stopped, waiting to see what he said.

“Ok, what was it about?” he asked.

She told him about her dream/vision/visit from Magne, the spirit god.

“So that’s what I was thinking about,” she said, after she had finished. “What do you think?”

“Hmm... Well, first of all, I can’t believe you held that in all through breakfast until now,” Zeus said with a frown, (or what counted as a frown for a tiger.) “Second of all, a visit from a spirit god? Magne, Magne. Hmm. Let me see.” He held up one of his paws, which had a silver bangle on it, and lifting it to his mouth, he breathed a plume of fire on a small flame shape that was etched there. “Close your eyes!” Zeus said urgently.

Athena had seen him do this before, and she’d once made the mistake of not listening to him, and the result had been a massive headache that had lasted for hours. So this time she obediently closed her eyes tightly.

There was a flash of light, then a small breeze, then all was still.

“Ok you can open them now,” Zeus said, in a gruff voice.

She slowly opened her eyes and blinked them several times, then finally settling them on the person now standing in front of her.

In human form, Zeus had auburn hair and green eyes, and he was six foot, two inches tall. He wore a short sleeved shirt, and loose pants with a belt that had a sword hanging from it. A small satchel was slung over his shoulder. On his back the two white wings were still there.

“Ah, there we go. That’s much better,” he said, stretching his arms above his head. “Being in tiger form all the time gets a little exhausting. And cramped,” he added.

“Well, thanks for the fantastic makeover, but how is this going to help us in any way with what we were talking about?” she asked. “Which was Magne, if you forgot,” she added.

“Okay, okay. Just a second,” he said. He cupped his hands over his mouth and yelled, “FAWNA!”

Barely two seconds later, a small fairy flew into the cave, and landed on his shoulder.

“I’m here,” said the fairy, who must be Fawna. “What do you need?” she asked.

“Who is Magne?”

Mysteries of Magne

"Magne, spirit god. She had a child, which was placed in the care of her sister, Elisha, a non-god, while Magne helped in the Great War. However, when Magne returned from the war, both Elisha and the child were nowhere to be found," Fawna stopped, her brown eyes bright. "However, there is more. Many people in a nearby village have reported seeing a woman who looked very similar to the sister, but the child has not been seen," Fawna said, fluttering her wings nervously. She looked at Athena with a puzzled expression on her face. "But…" she started, then shook her head.

Athena glanced at her, raising an eyebrow. Fawna sat down on Zeus's shoulder, and raised her eyebrow right back at Athena. Shocked, Athena's eyes widened and she laughed.

Zeus looked back and forth between them, confused, and then cleared his throat for attention.

"Well, now that you two have had your battle of wits, what next?" he asked, looking back and forth between Athena and Fawna.

Athena looked at Fawna, who shrugged her tiny shoulders, then at Zeus, who was staring intently at *her.* She closed her eyes and tried to think. *Well, there's no way to find out where the Grelgons are, and even if we did, it would take a long time to get there, if only I had wings! WAIT! There IS a way to find out where the Grelgons are.... I think,* Athena thought suddenly, her eyes flashing open. "There *is* a way to find out where the Grelgons are, but it might not do us any good, seeing as how I would not be able to keep up with you guys, what with your wings and all, but I guess I'll try it. I have to use this," she said, holding up her wrist, showing them the bracelet, the new charm twinkling.

The pair looked at her in synchronized puzzlement. *Oh, right,* Athena thought. She carefully explained about the bracelet and its significance. After she was done they were both nodding.

"Ok, so, let's just see how this goes, I guess," she said, bringing the bracelet close to her mouth. "Um, let's see.... aha! *Magne, Magne, come to me. I have a question to ask thee,*" she intoned.

Nothing happened, then a few seconds later there was a flash of light and a small gust of wind, swirling around with some sort of fog. Athena blinked, waiting for the fog to clear. As the mist disappeared, Athena noticed the figure standing there.

The Child

“Magne?” Athena asked.

“Yes.” Magne said, lifting her head, with a small smile.

Athena looked over and saw Zeus and Fawna looking at her expectantly.

“Wait, um...can they see you?” Athena asked.

“No, not unless I allow them to. However, if you trust them, I will let them see me,” Magne responded.

“I trust them. At least, I trust Zeus. But I do need their help with this, so I trust Fawna too,” Athena said quickly.

“Very well.” Magne said, snapping her fingers.

Zeus and Fawna jumped, as if breaking from a trance. They both stared wide-eyed at Magne, their expressions ranging from awe to outrage to a combination of both.

Sensing an altercation, Athena quickly jumped in before anything could happen. “Magne, this is Zeus and Fawna. Zeus, Fawna, this is Ma—”

“—I already know who she is,” Fawna said, crossing her tiny arms with a haughty expression.

“Um, okay then…. Anyway, Magne I have a question for yo—”

"So do I," Fawna interrupted, glaring at Magne.

"You do?" Magne and Athena asked in unison.

"Yes, why did you leave your child in the hands of your sister, who apparently was untrustworthy?" Fawna asked indignantly, raising an eyebrow.

"Um, I don't think—" Magne stopped, scrutinizing the little fairy. "Wait a minute, are you thinking it was my fault that my harebrained sister decided to run off with *MY* child? Because if you are, then little fairy—"

"—Fawna," the fairy said through clenched teeth.

"Then you've got another think coming, *Fawna*."

Fawna glared mutinously at Magne, scowling. "Tell me this then, *where is the child*?"

"I-I don't know..." Magne said, rather guiltily. "And even if I did know, it's none of your business!" she shot back.

"STOP! Stop!" Athena ordered, placing herself between the two. "You're both acting like children! No fighting!" she said warily.

She looked over and caught Zeus trying to contain a smile, his green eyes amused. *What, exactly, is so funny about this?* Athena thought, annoyed. *Ok, whatever, let's try this, AGAIN!* She took a deep breath.

"Magne, if I could *please* ask my question now?"

"Yes, of course," Magne said, calmly.

"Ok, actually, I have two questions…." Athena said slowly. *I actually kind of want to know about the child too,* she thought.

"Yes?" Magne said impatiently.

"Ok, where are the Grelgons right now?" she asked.

"They are halfway to Runespire Forest, though why they are headed that way, I do not know. Now, your next question?" Magne asked politely.

"Right, um whatever I ask you, you'll answer it no matter what…right?" Athena asked hesitantly.

Magne narrowed her eyes in suspicion. "Yes…" she said tentatively.

"Okay, then who is the child and do you know where it is, for real?" Athena asked.

Fawna's scowl disappeared, and she perked up, alert, waiting to hear Magne's answer. "Seriously?" Magne said, "you're going to waste your question on *that*?"

"Yes, and you said you would answer…" Athena said, shoot Magne a *get-on-with-it* look. "And I don't see what's so bad about the question. I just—*we*," she corrected herself. "*We* just want to know where the child is…what's so bad abou—"

"You!" Magne blurted.

Athena stopped, confused. "Me? What did I d—"

"No! *You!* It's *you!* The *child* is *you*, Athena, or should I say, *daughter*."

If Magne had said something else, Athena didn't hear her, because that was when everything started to fade…

A Mothers' Memories

Athena tried to ignore the voices. But they were so *insistent*. They wouldn't stop.

"Wake up!"

"Athena? Athena, wake up!"

"Daughter? Athena?"

That last one, it couldn't be could it? But who else would it be? Oh well, she couldn't ignore them forever, not unless she had some sort of magical power…. WAIT!

Athena sat upright so fast, her head started to spin, and she winced at the pain, slowly laying back down. Once her eyes had adjusted to the light, she looked around at the worried faces above her. One by one, they came into focus.

"Athena? Thank *Lithra*! You scared me!" Zeus said gently. "Don't ever do that again!" he added firmly.

"Oh, good, you're ok! I was really worried," Fawna said nervously.

"I'm sorry…I should have told you sooner," Magne said, burying her face in her hands. "I just, I didn't know what to do. I was scared that you wouldn't want me to be your mother, or that you would not accept me because I'm a god," Magne explained, her voice muffled by her hands.

"Mag—Mother, it's okay." Athena said quietly. She discreetly shot Zeus a give-us-a-minute look. He nodded and motioned for Fawna to follow him. Fawna hesitated, opening her mouth as if to say something, then shook her head and flew after Zeus, following him out of the cave.

"Mother?" Athena asked gently.

Magne looked up with tears in her eyes, and it was then that the memories returned.

She was alone on a battlefield, wreckage everywhere, no one else around. "Hello?" she called out, but there was no answer. "What th–" Athena started to say, then stopped as a blinding pain shot through her head. *She was walking through piles of rubble. The mournful peal of a long forgotten church bell echoed throughout the cold abandoned village.* "Ow–" *She was looking down at the tiny child in her arms, trying to engrave the memory of its' young innocent face into her mind, before passing the child to her watchful sister.* "Stop..please.." Athena whispered, her head pounding.

Only you can make it stop, Athena. Control it. Embrace it. Fear it. Hear it. For it holds the key to who you truly are.

Flying and Flailing

Athena looked at the map, then at the sky, then at the map again.

"Awesome plan, but there's just one thing missing," she said to Zeus.

"Oh, yeah?" he asked, raising an eyebrow. "And what might that be?"

"How are we supposed to get from *here* to *there*," she pointed to the mark on the map, "when I can't fly?" *I wish,* she thought.

"That's easy!" he answered, his green eyes twinkling. "We carry you!"

▪▪▪▪▪

Ten minutes later she was soaring through the clouds, wind whipping through her hair.

"This is fun!" she said to Zeus, "but what about when you get tired?"

"I have a plan, don't worry!" he replied.

Twenty minutes later, Zeus passed Athena off to Magne. Athena thought it was still kind of weird to call her "mom", seeing as she'd only just learned that yesterday. Or two days ago. Or maybe it was yesterday. She couldn't remember. *Wow, I can't even remember* that, *but apparently I can 'remember' memories that aren't even mine,* she thought with a wry smile.

▪▪▪▪▪

Several trade-offs later, they were on the ground again, sitting beside a small stream. After filling her canteen and drinking what she could, Athena refilled it and twisted the cap tightly shut, placing it in her bag.

"Well, great plan," Athena said, walking over to Zeus, "but now what?" she asked, bumping his arm with her elbow. "Mr. Genius," she added playfully.

Zeus grinned. "Just a sec," he said, bumping her with his elbow. "Be right back," he said, standing up.

Athena watched him walk over to Fawna, who was sitting on a small rock, apparently talking to a…*wait a minute*…is that a…ladybug? Athena shook her head, smiling. She watched Zeus ask Fawna something, which caused the fairy's face to scrunch up in concentration. Then she nodded, and smiled. After saying something to the ladybug, Fawna joined Zeus as he walked back over to Athena. Athena smiled at them.

"Well?" she asked.

"Fawna here is going to sprinkle you with fairy dust, which will allow you to fly, though only for a limited amount of time," Zeus explained.

"Oh! Cool!" Athena said, excited. "So no more carrying?"

"Exactly."

"Cool, so when can we do it? Right now?" *I've always wondered what it would be like to fly! Not by being carried, but on your own,* she thought excitedly.

"Probably not. It's almost noon, and I'm very hungry–" he stopped, grinning as he saw her already growing scowl deepen. "I'm just kidding! Yeah, sure we can do it now, I guess. Fawna?" Zeus asked, still smiling.

Fawna stuck a hand into the tiny bag slung over her shoulder, pulling it out full of a shimmery silver colored powder. She motioned for Athena to hold out her hand, and when she did, the fairy poured the powder into it.

"Now, take it and sprinkle it on top of your head," Fawna instructed.

Athena sprinkled the powder over herself, and immediately felt herself start to float. She grinned at Zeus.

"There, now you are good to go! But remember, it only lasts for *2 hours*, so be careful!" Zeus warned.

"Don't worry, I'll be fine!" she said, then she grinned, and leaned forward, punching him on the arm. "Tag, you're it!" she said gleefully, shooting off into the air.

▪▪▪▪▪

Athena was soaring through the air, the wind whistling in her ears, her hair getting tossed around. *This is so cool! I love flying!* she thought. She looked down at the ground far below her, spotting the small fire flickering, the light shining on the three figures sitting around the flames. There they were, *sitting*, whereas *she* was going to be *flying*, because she didn't want to waste a single *second* of her time that was left from the powder. She flew in dizzying spirals and loop-de-loops, loving her newfound freedom.

Suddenly, she felt herself drop a foot closer to the ground. Then two feet. *Oh no! The time! It's running out!* She looked around frantically for the orange glow of the fire, finding none. Slowly she dropped foot-by-foot until suddenly she started to fall, the ground speeding up to meet her. She cried out, then spiraled down, down, down, disappearing into the thicket of overgrown weeds.

Nothing, Except Everything

Zeus was worried. Athena should have been back by now. She should have been back *two hours* ago. *Oh no! Two hours! The fairy dust!* He quickly stood up, looking around. Magne and Fawna looked at him quizzically.

"Where is Athena?" he asked. "She should have been back by now," he said urgently.

Fawna sat up straight, her eyes frightened. "Oh no!" she squeaked. "The fairy dust! You warned her about it, right?" she asked, her eyes as wide as the moon.

"Yes," he said, "but it must have caught her by surprise."

Zeus shot up into the sky, searching the ground below him for any signs.

"Athena! ATHENA!" he shouted, "WHERE ARE YOU?"

He looked down and spotted a speck of white alone in the black sea of grass. He dipped closer and saw that it was a feather. With a bit of green at the tip. WAIT! His mind flashed back to when they had first met up and went to the cave. Athena's arrows! They were fletched with feathers, white with green on them, exactly like this one! He instantly dropped to the ground, and started to rip away at the thicket.

"Athena! Athena!" Zeus cried with renewed energy.

He finally made it to the center of the brambles and stared in disbelief at what lay before him.

There was nothing. All that flying, searching, digging, and here he was, and there was *nothing*.

Nothing, except for time and space….

Nothing, except for the ground and the sky….

Nothing, except for the sound of silence….

Nothing…. except for a bow and a quiver of arrows.

Winging It

Athena slowly woke to the sound of voices. Her head was pounding and the continuous stream of voices around her did not help.

"What is *it*?"

"I think *it* is called a *man-who*?"

"No. A *human*. And *it* has ears. *It* can hear."

Athena slowly opened one eye, then the other, squinting at the brightness of the light shining in her face. She stared at the canvas above her, trying to regain her sense of mobility. Slowly, she lifted her head, looking around. She was in a tent, she guessed, based on the ceiling fabric and the shape of the walls. She looked over and saw what appeared to be a creature with two pointy ears, a sharp nose, and a scary looking amount of fang-shaped teeth. And its…skin…its skin was..*green.* Athena gasped, suddenly realizing she knew what the creature was. Her mind flashed back to when Zeus was telling her about the Grelgons he'd seen in the woods. *Grelgons! Oh no! What have I done?* Athena thought, tears brimming in her eyes.

The Grelgons looked at her with puzzled expressions on their faces. Then they looked at each other and shrugged.

Wait, she thought, confused. *That must mean, I'm in a Grelgon camp? Oh no, I hope the queen is not here,* she thought, thinking about the evil Grelgon ruler, Queen Lanthiraya. A sharp pain shot across her wrist and she looked down, confusion and wonder clouding her face as she saw that her wrist had been put in a splint, and her ribs had been bandaged.

There was also something, something on her back…and it hurt. She twisted herself around, trying to see what was wrong with her back, and she stopped, awestruck as she stared at the wings on her back.

Wings! She had *wings*! She blinked, half expecting this to be a dream, and the wings to vanish. But, no! Each time she opened her eyes, the two gray feathery wings were still there. She slowly stood up, stretching them as far as she could.

Wings! I have wings! Oh! Just wait until I can tell Zeus! she thought, then stopped. *Wait, but where am I*?

"Excuse me?" she croaked. "Where am I?"

"IT speaks!" a Grelgon cried, running out of the tent.

"Of course it speaks!" said another Grelgon, rolling its eyes. "You are in a Grelgon camp, human," it said to Athena.

"Yes, I can see that but where? Like where are we in Fuamahoya?" she asked.

"Somewhere near Ethrulcath," he responded.

"Oh, ok. Um, am I able to leave?" she asked.

"Of course! We are not stopping you from leaving," he said with a toothy smile. "But first, come and get some food."

Athena grabbed her cloak from where it lay on a nearby chair, and spying her bag, she snatched it up, slinging it over her shoulder. She searched the tent for her bow, but couldn't find it.

"Excuse me, um..where are my bow and arrows?"

"Oh..we..um..left them where we found you…Sorry."

"Oh well, I can find them when I leave." *I hope.* Athena feigned a smile, hoping it looked real. "Show me around."

"Ok." said the Grelgon. "Follow me to the kitchen," he said, then scrunched up his nose, "though, it hardly qualifies as a kitchen," he added.

▪▪▪▪▪

Twenty minutes later, Athena was sitting in front of the fire, laughing at a joke that the nice Grelgon, whose name was Gykemi, had told. She would have loved to stay there longer, but she had more important, pressing things to attend to. Such as saving Fuamahoya from impending doom.

I have a kingdom to save.

Reunion

Zeus stood on the hill, studying the camp below him, watching the cloaked figure sitting by the fire laugh merrily. He looked closer at her and noticed a small…bump? No, wait, *two bumps.* Athena threw her head back, laughing, and her cloak shifted, revealing something feathery on her back. *Wings?* Zeus thought, his eyes widening.

He leaped into the air and gave two powerful pumps of his wings, flying high above the camp. He hovered overhead, scrutinizing the figures moving around below him. They weren't holding Athena against her will, so….

He aimed downward, pulling his wings in so he went into a nosedive. Ten feet from the ground, he snapped his wings open and with a soft *thump*, he landed in the middle of the camp. Startled faces peered at him through the dying light. Athena whirled around, and her face lit up.

"Zeus!" she cried, running towards him.

"Athena," he said, enveloping her in a tight hug. "I'm so glad you're ok."

She looked him in the face, and a slow smile spread across her face, and she pulled him to her in another hug.

“I have WINGS!” she whispered, excitedly. “For REAL.”

“Let me see,” he said, anxious. *If she is the daughter of a god, then she is a half-god, so wings are* probably *not going to be the extent of her abilities,* he thought. *But we still don’t yet know who the father is…*

Athena pulled off her cloak, revealing the two feathery gray wings on her back. Zeus stretched out one of his own, brushing it against one of hers. A strange tingling feeling went through him as the two made contact.

“Zeus, I have *so much* to tell you,” Athena said, gazing into his eyes.

“Well, I suppose maybe you should wait, so you don't have to repeat yourself,” he replied, motioning to the sky.

Two figures were slowly gliding down, landing on the grass with soft *thumps*.

“So,” said Magne, a twinkle in her eye. “You’ve grown your wings.”

Fight and Flight

Athena stared in shock at her mother. Fawna backed away, mumbling something, then flew off. Athena watched her go, then turned back to her mother.

"You *knew*?" she said incredulously.

"Of course I knew," Magne replied with a wave of her hand. "I mean, it's not a surprise, if both parents have wings, the chance of the child having wings is nearly 100 percent, and given who your father is—" she cut herself off, shuffling her feet.

"My father? Who is my father?" Athena asked, giving her mother a critical look.

"Oh, um...never mind. Just forget I said anything," Magne said nervously.

"Why is it such a big *deal*?" Athena huffed, crossing her arms. "Can't you *at least* give me his *name*?" she prodded.

"No, because that would tell you *exactly* who he is…" Magne said impatiently. "Please just forget I said anything about it, ok?" she said, irritated. She turned and stormed off in a very un-godlike manner.

Athena started to go after her, but Zeus grabbed her arm and shook his head. He tentatively wrapped his wing around her and she flinched at the sudden contact, then leaned farther into his warmth.

"Don't go after her. It'll only make things worse," he whispered, "give her some time to cool down."

"I just wanted to know his *name*. What's so bad about that?" she whispered back, her voice muffled as she buried her head in his shoulder. He smelled good. Like wood, and cinnamon.

"I don't know." Zeus admitted. "Maybe she thinks that knowing the truth will hurt you more than not knowing at all," he murmured.

"Zeus, I'm so confused. I don't know what to do about the Grelgons, I don't know what is happening to me, and I don't even know who I even am. I just wish—"

"Shh," he shushed her, putting a finger on her lips. "Calm down. Let's go sit down and talk, and then you need to rest," he said, looking into her eyes.

"Ok, yeah. Sleep sounds good," she said tiredly.

"Let's go then," he said, then he grinned. "race ya to the tent," he said mischievously, jumping into the air and circling over her before zooming away.

Athena laughed and shot into the air, a bit wobbly, as she'd not used her wings before now. But she flew strong and gracefully as she raced to keep up with her care-free friend.

"I'm gonna catch you!" she shouted, laughing, the wind whipping her hair around.

“Eat my dust!” he called back, grinning. “You’ll NEVER catch me!” he taunted.

Athena laughed and flew faster, feeling like the ruler of the sky. Feeling powerful, and strong. Feeling like the god of the world. *Who knows?* she thought. *Maybe I AM a god.*

Gone

Athena sipped at her steaming mug of cocoa, her cold fingers gratefully absorbing the heat emanating from the cup.

Zeus sat across from her, gazing out the skylight on the ceiling of the tent, occasionally taking sips of his drink, his head in space.

Suddenly, a commotion outside caused the two to jump up, their focus shifting to the door flap, which was hastily flung open by a Grelgon guard, who had a frown on his face.

“Miss, there is a messenger here to see you, apparently about your mother,” he said in a bored tone. “Would you like me to—”

“Yes, yes!” Athena said hurriedly. “Let him in!”

The flap opened wider and a smaller Grelgon burst in, running to Athena. He flung himself at her feet, his face terrified.

“Miss…there’s been an incident…. your...mother….” he explained breathlessly. “It... all happened…so fast...”

“What is it? What’s happened?” Athena asked urgently.

“It’s your mother…. she’s been kidnapped.”

Brave

Athena could hardly believe what she was hearing. *Kidnapped*, she thought. Her mother was kidnapped, missing, *gone*. She couldn't help but think about how it was probably her fault, maybe if she hadn't have pushed so hard about wanting to know who her father was, maybe her mother would've been here right now.

The rustle of fabric near her ear made Athena jump. Zeus backed away, raising his hands in an "I come in peace" gesture. She let out the breath caught in her throat and sighed, sitting down on the chair.

"Stop. *Stop*." Zeus said, giving her a stern look.

"What?" she mumbled.

"I see you, giving up, blaming yourself. Stop it. It's not your fault and you know it," he said, crouching down to look her in the eyes. "We *both* know it," he added firmly.

"But—"

"No." Zeus said sternly. "We are not going to sit around and dwell on this, and keep thinking about how it was our fault and how we could've stopped it. We are going to be brave, and strong so we can find your mother," he said, his eyes never leaving hers. "Starting now."

Information

Zeus stood staring at the thicket, half-expecting something to jump out and grab him. Shivering, he tried to shake off the uneasy feeling. He put on a "I'm fine, thank you" face and turned toward the guard.

"You're absolutely sure on what you saw?" he asked in a serious tone.

"Yes, sir. I saw the goddess sitting right 'ere," he said, moving to stand at a spot to the right of Athena. "An' then some Grelgons jumped out, they was no ordinary Grelgons, they was some o' those evil ones that follow Queen Lanthiraya. Anyhow, they were hidin' in them there weeds, an' I saw 'em jump out an' take 'er. They was gone in a second," he said, snapping his fingers. "Like that. Or I woulda wen' after 'em," he added.

Zeus narrowed his eyes at the guard. "Did you see where they went?" he asked.

"Nope. Like I said, they was 'ere one second, gone the next, else I woulda stopped 'em o' course," he added.

Zeus huffed, irritated. He wanted to storm off and think about things, but he couldn't because he had to stay strong for Athena, and anyways, he still had one more question for the guard.

“Did you recognize any of them?” he asked, already thinking about what the answer might be.

To his surprise, the guard nodded. “Uh-huh. In fact, one of ’em was an ol’ buddy o’ mine, from the way back days when I believed in following Lanthiraya. Anyhow, ’is names Gilleon. Don’ know ’bout dem other ones tho’, ’cept I knows they is some o’ the Queens own guards. But thas’ all I know,” the guard said.

“Thank you, that helped us a lot,” Zeus said, reaching into his satchel and pulling out a small bag. Metal clinked together as he reached in and pulled out several silver coins, handing them to the guard. “Thank you for your time,” he said.

The guards’ eyes widened. “Thank ye’,” he whispered, closing his fingers tightly over the coins.

Zeus nodded and turned to face Athena. “Let’s go find Fawna, maybe she can help us,” he said. Athena nodded.

They walked all through the camp, stopping at each tent to look in or ask anyone if they had seen a small fairy, but without luck.

They stopped at a small campfire, and asked the Grelgons around it if they had seen the fairy and one nodded and pointed to a small green tent, set apart from the rest. Zeus and Athena thanked him, and walked in that direction. They reached the tent and pulled the flap open, stepping inside. Once their eyes had adjusted to the light, they looked around. A small table was set up in the center, and Fauna was hovering over it, scrutinizing the chessboard laid out on it. After a few minutes, she dropped down, picked up the queen and flew the piece across the board, where she placed it on the opposite side, displacing the carved king sitting there.

"Checkmate!" she cried joyfully, doing flips in the air.

Zeus and Athena exchanged amused expressions, then Zeus stepped forward and cleared his throat.

Fawna spun around. "Zeus! I won! Now I'm the chess champion!" she cried, pumping her tiny fists in the air.

"I see that," Zeus said. "But can the chess champion come help us with something?"

"Sure!" said Fawna. "Where's Magne?" she asked, looking around.

"Well, um…that's actually what we need your help with…" Athena said. "She's… um…she's been kidnapped."

Frightened Fairy

"What?!" Fawna cried. "How? When?"

The two quickly explained what happened after Fawna had flown off, and everything they had found out from the Grelgon guard. By the time they had finished, Fawna was shaking with rage.

"So, um…do you think you might know where she is? Or even who might have her?" Athena asked gently.

"Of course I know!" the fairy cried, hysterical. "The queen of the Grelgons has her, and she probably wants you guys too!"

Mindspeak

Athena listened to the hum of voices around her. She was sitting cross-legged on a rug on the ground, her eyes closed. She tried to tune out the sounds around her, trying to summon something, any shred of power she might have that she didn't know about. All of a sudden, she heard a whisper in her head. *Focus, Athena, focus. Believe in yourself, or all is lost.* Athena's eyes flew open. She *knew* that voice.

Mother? Athena whispered back, *is that you?*

Yes, Magne's voice replied.

Oh! Are you alright? The guards, they said you were…taken…kidnapped…godnapped, whatever you call it.

Athena heard a wry chuckle and then heard Magne speak:

Yes, I guess you could say I was 'godnapped'. Magne sighed a mental sigh. *But you can't worry about that right now. You need to focus on the task at hand.*

Right, Athena said. *Um…what exactly would that be? Apart from, you know, saving you from evil Grelgons?*

Well, they're not evil. *Just the queen is.* Magne said defensively.

Wait! You've seen *the queen? What does she look like?*

Magne let out a laugh. *No, silly. Of course I haven't seen the queen. All I've seen, so far, Is the outskirts of the Grelgon camp, and the inside of this tent. Here, I'll show you...*

Athena heard a low hum and then she saw an image appear in her mind. A small tent, with a rug, a lamp, and a small cot in the corner.

As you can see, it's not exactly 5-star worthy. But it's not bad, Magne thought wryly. *Don't get jealous, though.*

Athena laughed, with both her mind and voice. Zeus glanced over at her, giving her a curious look, which made her laugh more. Puzzled, he stood up and walked over to her.

"What are you laughing about?" he asked, raising an eyebrow.

"I'm laughing at what Magne said," she stated simply. "I'm talking to her."

"*Really*?" he breathed, his eyes widening. "How?"

Athena was about to respond, when Magne whispered a word to her. "*Mindspeak.*"

Faeuna

"*Mindspeak*? What is *that*?" Zeus asked, eyes wide.

"Its…its where..." she stopped, listening to Magne explain it to her.

It's a secret power that gods and some half-gods have, where they can enter each other's minds and speak to one another as easily as if they were having a conversation face-to-face, like you are right now, Magne explained.

Athena repeated what Magne had said, out loud, for Zeus to hear.

"*Oh*! That's cool. Can Magne hear me?" he asked.

"I don't—" Athena stopped as Magne spoke to her, in her mind.

Yes, I can hear him, but only through you.

"Yes, she can hear you, but only through me…" Athena repeated.

But, that does not matter. Athena, you must listen to me, I need to tell you about your secret power, Magne said urgently.

"*Secret what? Secret power? I have one of those?*" she asked with both mind and voice.

Yes. Now, do you remember how Zeus can transform into a tiger

Uh...yeah...why?

Because, you can too...well...not into a tiger, *yours should be a wolf, at least, I think so...*

What do you mean? What are you talking about?

Your 'Faeuna' or 'spirit animal', what you truly *are, or would be, if you were an animal instead of human,* Magne said impatiently. *On your forearm, your* right *forearm, you have a tattoo of a wolf paw.*

What? No! when would I have...Oh! She gasped as she looked at the small but clearly visible wolf paw print on her forearm. *Ok, I guess I have one...but how does that help me?*

If you want to shapeshift into your Faeuna form, all you have to do is whisper the word 'wyshu' to the paw print and...well...just do it and find out. I have to go, they are approaching my tent and I don't want them to find out I'm talking to you, that could put you in danger.

"*Um, ok,*" Athena said as a buzzing noise filled her head, then vanished.

"Is she gone?" Zeus asked.

"Yes," Athena said, somewhat glumly.

"What was all that about? What did she talk to you about?" he asked, his eyes filled with curiosity.

"Well, apparently, I have a 'Faeuna' that I can transform into…so, let's try this, shall we?"

She brought her arm up, holding the tattoo close to her lips, and whispered to it. "*Wyshu.*"

All of a sudden, she felt as if she were weightless. She closed her eyes, hearing a low humming in her head. She felt a breeze pick up, rotating around her. Then, a flash of bright light. Even with her eyes closed, she could still see the flash of bright light through her eyelids. It was the same thing that happened when Zeus did it. After a moment, the breeze started to die down, and then everything went still…

Heart of a Wolf

One minute Zeus saw Athena standing in front of him, mist swirling around her. The next minute, he saw a gray wolf standing in front of him, icy blue eyes looking into his. Two grayish black wings were on its back, the feathers swaying in the dying breeze.

"Athena?" Zeus whispered.

"Did it work?" the wolf asked.

"Yes. I mean, I suppose so, seeing as how there is now a wolf standing in front of me instead of a human," he said with a laugh.

"I want to see," she said. "I wish I could see myself."

"I think…hold on," he said, "I have an idea."

He walked over to the kitchen tent, grabbing a cauldron. Then he walked over to the river, dipping the cauldron in, pulling it out, full to the brim. Step-by-step, he carefully walked back over to her, setting the makeshift mirror in front of her. "There," he said.

Athena stepped forward, and studied her reflection. "Wow," she whispered, her breath creating tiny ripples on the water. "This is…awesome…"

"Yes, it is…um…I would *love* to let you just stand there and stare at yourself all day, but um…we have more important things to do…such as…for instance…saving your mother…" he said.

Athena glanced one last time at her reflection, then sighed and reversed the transformation so she was once again in human form, standing in front of Zeus.

"You're right, we have to help her. But first, let's get Fawna," she said. "And tell her *everything*.

To the Rescue

They summoned the fairy and quickly explained all that had happened.

"I can't believe that you guys did that without me!" Fawna whined.

"Well, we aren't going to be able to save Magne without your help," Athena pointed out.

"Oh, yeah! That's right! Okay, we can do this! Let's save Magne!" she said, her eyes bright. "TO MAGNE!" she shouted.

"TO MAGNE!" Zeus and Athena shouted in unison, earning curious looks from the Grelgons scattered in the camp.

We're coming, Mother, Athena thought fiercely. *We'll find you and rescue you, and then save Fuamahoya. The fate of the future depends on us.*

End of Book 1:

The Fate of the Future

Fayesh

In Fuamahoya, there is a language that gods and half-gods, and some others speak. It is called *Fayesh*, and its words are not only sacred, but also have power, if used correctly. Along with having names for objects, the language also has names for people.

There is some speculation on whether this language is corrupted or not. Some say it should be kept and revised to be better understood. Others say the Faylean gods should abolish the language entirely, along with those who use it. Listed on the next page is a dictionary/pronunciation guide for your benefit, to help you better understand the words in this revered language.

Pronunciation Guide and Glossary

Athena – (uh-thee-nuh): Daughter of Magne (see: Magne); Zeus' best friend (see: Zeus)

Dract-Nate – (dr-act-nay-t): Death City; literally "city of death"

Drelfo-Nalta – (drel-foe-nal-tuh): Death Land; the smaller of the two land masses that make up the continent of Fuamahoya; it is ruled by the queen of the Grelgons (see: Lanthiraya)

Ethrulcath – (ehth-rule-cath): Eternal Castle

Faeuna – (fay-oo-nuh): spirit animal

Fayesh – (fay-esh): ancient language that the people of Fuamahoya used to speak, many centuries ago

Faylean – (fay-lee-an): a race of human-like beings that have mysterious powers and god-like abilities

Ferthshan – (furth-shawn): Fortune Island

Freshnu-Gahnda – (fresh-new-g-on-duh): land of plenty; the biggest of the land masses that make up Fuamahoya

Fuamahoya – (foo-ahm-uh-hoy-uh): land of the beginning; believed to be the first place on Earth that the Faylean gods stepped foot on; a large continent in the Eastern Sea that is split into two countries: Freshnu-Gahnda (see: Freshnu-Gahnda) and Drelfo-Nalta (see: Drelfo-Nalta)

Fydragt –(fy-dract): “Fire Fury”; the Fayesh name for the volcano on the Grelgon part of Fuamahoya (see: Drelfo-Nalta)

Grelgon – (grel-gun): a half-elf, half-gorgon creature that has green skin, pointy ears, pointed nose, and sharp fang-like teeth

Gre – (gr-ee): The Fayesh word for “tree”

Gren – (gr-en): The Fayesh word for “trees” or “forest”

Grenshan – (gren-shawn): island of trees/forests; literally “tree island”

Gykemi – (guy-key-me): Grelgon whom Athena befriends

Hitru-gren –(hi-true-gren): “the hidden forest”

Ilgletan – (ilg-lee-tan): cluster of egg shaped islands off the northern coast of Freshnu-Gahnda; literally “basket of eggs”

Lanthiraya – (lan-thi-ray-uh): Queen of the Grelgons

Lithlanya – (lith-l-an-yuh): "lifeline"; a river that splits from the Venleatuan to go through Hitru-Gren and across Rehaventna

Lithra – (lih-thr-uh): goddess of light/life

Magne –(mag-knee): spirit god/goddess; Athena's mother

Mudek – (moo-deck): island between Grenshan and Wenshawten; literally "the one in the middle"

Rehaventna – (re-have-ent-nuh): a mountain range along the western coast of Freshnu-Gahnda; made up of a bunch of tall pointed spires of rock; literally "the pointed rocks"

Renthykians – (wren-thyk-ee-ans): old Fayesh name for Grelgons (see: Grelgons)

Senthra – (sen-thruh): a small village at the southern base of Rehaventna; literally "the village of safety"

Tygru –(tie-grew): old Fayesh name for "tiger"

Venleatuan – (ven-lee-uh-to-on): a great river chasm that splits the continent of Freshnu-Gahnda (bigger part of Fuamahoya) in half; literally "the crack in the stone"

Wyshu – (why-shoo): old Fayesh name for "wolf"

Zeus – (z-oos): Athena's best friend (see: Athena)

Made in the USA
Middletown, DE
16 April 2022

64121322R00040